Robert Burns, Henry Arthur Bright

Some Account of the Glenriddell Mss. of Burns's Poems

With Several Poems Never Before Published

Robert Burns, Henry Arthur Bright

Some Account of the Glenriddell Mss. of Burns's Poems
With Several Poems Never Before Published

ISBN/EAN: 9783337124007

Printed in Europe, USA, Canada, Australia, Japan

Cover: Foto ©Andreas Hilbeck / pixelio.de

More available books at **www.hansebooks.com**

SOME ACCOUNT

OF

THE GLENRIDDELL MSS

OF

BURNS'S POEMS:

WITH SEVERAL POEMS NEVER BEFORE PUBLISHED.

EDITED BY

HENRY A. BRIGHT.

[Printed for Private Distribution.]

LIVERPOOL:

GILBERT G. WALMSLEY, 50, LORD STREET.

1874.

CONTENTS.

———◦—◦———

PREFACE.

In 1853 the widow of Mr. Wallace Currie (son of Dr. Currie, the biographer of Burns) presented to the Athenæum Library, Liverpool, two curious and interesting manuscript volumes. They are thus described in the Athenæum Catalogue :—

" Poems written by Mr. Robert Burns, and selected by him from his unprinted collection for Robert Riddell, of Glenriddell, Esq. A quarto volume of 162 pages, exclusive of portrait, title, and an introductory letter. The letter, and seventy-eight pages of the poems, are entirely in the poet's autograph. The rest of the MS. is in the handwriting of amanuenses, with occasional corrections and remarks by Burns himself."

" Letters by Mr. Burns, which he selected for R. Riddell, Esq., of Glenriddell, F.A.S. of London and Edinr., and Member of the Literary and Philosophical Society of Manchester. A quarto volume, containing 103 pages, exclusive of title and portrait. The first six pages are blank; the rest of the volume is in Burns's autograph."

Until last year these volumes had been so carefully preserved under lock and key, that very few even of the proprietors of the Athenæum knew of their existence. At my suggestion, they have now been placed within a glass case in the library, and may at all times be readily inspected.

The volume of letters contains some unpublished matter, most of which was sent by me to the *Athenæum*, of Aug. 1, 1874.

The volume of poems I have carefully examined and collated with the Kilmarnock edition, and with that of Mr. Alexander Smith.

On the fly-leaf at the beginning are the arms of Mr. Riddell, and a portrait of Burns. On the title-page is the inscription, " Poems written by Mr. Robert Burns, and selected by him from his unprinted collection, for Robert Riddell, of Glenriddell, Esq.;" and then follow ten lines of verse about Burns,

> " Here native genius, gay, unique, and strong,
> Shines through each page, and marks the tuneful song :
> Wrapt Admiration her warm tribute pays,
> And Scotia proudly echoes all she says :
> Bold Independence too, illumes the theme,
> And claims a manly privilege to Fame.
> Vainly, O Burns! would rank or riches shine,
> Compar'd with inborn merit great as thine ;
> These chance may take, as chance has often giv'n ;
> But pow'rs like thine can only come from heav'n."

After this, the book, as Burns left it, begins.

There is first a preface in his own handwriting, which deprecates the publication of these poems. With or without the poet's permission, however, almost everything the book contains

has long since been given to the world, and the few things that
Dr. Currie omitted, mainly on account of their political bias,
may now at last be allowed to "see the light."

The preface is as follows :—

" As this Collection almost wholly consists of pieces local or unfinished, fragments
the effusion of a poetical moment and bagatelles strung in rhyme simply *pour
passer le temps*, the Author trusts that nobody into whose hands it may come
will without his permission give, or allow to be taken, copies of anything here
contained ; much less to give to the world at large, what he never meant
should see the light.   At the Gentleman's request, whose from this time it
shall be, the Collection was made ; and to him, and I will add, to his amiable
Lady, it is presented, as a sincere though small tribute of gratitude for the many
many happy hours the Author has spent under their roof.   *There*, what Poverty
even though accompanied with Genius must seldom expect to meet with at the
tables and in the circles of Fashionable Life, his welcome has ever been, The
cordiality of Kindness and the warmth of Friendship.   As from the situation in
which it is now placed, this MSS. may be preserved, and this Preface read,
when the hand that now writes and the heart that now dictates it may be moulder-
ing in the dust ; let these be regarded as the genuine sentiments of a man
who seldom flattered any, and never those he loved.

" ROBᵗ   BURNS.

" 27TH APRIL, 1791."

Of the poems I give a complete catalogue, transcribing in full
such as are unpublished.   The titles, and any notes *before*
the first line, are exactly as they appear in the MSS.   Notes
which I have added are distinguished by brackets [ ].   No alteration of any sort has been made in Burns's spelling or punctuation.

I must leave it to others to criticise these unpublished poems, and to show that, if of unequal merit, they have still their value and their interest. My own task has been to gather up, carefully as I could, what are probably the last fragments, which are ever likely to be printed, of the great poet's verse. It remains only that I should express my obligation to Mr. Scott Douglas of Edinburgh, (who is, perhaps, the best living authority on all matters connected with Burns,) for the valuable information he has given me, and for the account of Riddell of Glenriddell, which he has kindly furnished.

HENRY A. BRIGHT.

LIVERPOOL, *October*, 1874.

Catalogue of the Poems.

I.

Song—Tune " Bonie Dundee."

> " In Mauchline there dwells six proper young Belles."

In Burns's autograph.

Note added by Burns—

> " Note, Miss Armour is now known by the designation of Mrs. Burns."

II.

Song.

> " Anna, thy charms my bosom fire."

In Burns's autograph.

III.

Epistle to John Goldie, in Kilmarnock, author of The Gospel Recovered.   August, 1785.

> " O Gowdie, terror o' the whigs."

In Burns's autograph.

> [In this poem are two unpublished stanzas, two stanzas published as a separate piece, and various readings ;— I therefore transcribe it as it stands.]

B

IV.

To Miss Jeany Cruikshank, a very young lady, only child of my much esteemed friend, Mr. Cruikshank, of the High School, Edinbᵣ Written on the blank leaf of a book presented to her by the Author.

"Beauteous Rose-bud, young and gay."

In Burns's autograph.

[There is a variation in the second line,

" Blooming on *the early day*."]

V

Written on Friar's Carse Hermitage.

" Thou whom chance may hither lead."

In Burns's autograph.

[This is the *first version* of this well known poem.]

VI

On Captⁿ Grose's peregrinations through Scotland, collecting the Antiquities of that kingdom.

" Hear, Land o' Cakes, and brither Scots."

In Burns's autograph.

VII.

Ode to the departed Regency-Bill, 1789.

" Daughter of Chaos' doting years."

In Burns's autograph.

[Unpublished, and here transcribed.]

VIII.

Alteration of the Poem, page 6th [V.].

" Thou whom chance may hither lead."

In Burns's autograph.

IX.

Song—Tune, Banks of Banna.

" Yestreen I had a pint o' wine."

In Burns's autograph.

[In line 5, over the " *hungry Jew*," is written, the " *Israelite.*   The poem has here only two stanzas, but a note adds—

" For an additional stanza to this song, see page 26."—*Vide* XIII.]

X.

Song.

" I murder hate by field or flood."

In Burns's autograph.

[This has a second unpublished stanza, beginning—

" I would not die like Socrates,
For all the fuss of Plato ;
Nor would I with Leonidas,
Nor yet would I with Cato."]

XI.

Holy Willie's Prayer.

> "And send the godly in a pet to pray."—Pope.

Argument.

Holy Willie was a rather oldish batchelor Elder in the Parish of Mauchline, and much and justly famed for that polemical chattering which ends in tippling Orthodoxy, and for that Spiritualized Bawdry which refines to Liquorish Devotion. In a sessional process with a gentleman in Mauchline, a Mr. Gavin Hamilton, Holy Willie, and his priest, father Auld, after full hearing in the Presbytry of Ayr, came off but second best; owing partly to the oratorical powers of Mr. Robᵗ Aiken, Mr. Hamilton's Counsel; but chiefly to Mr. Hamilton's being one of the most irreproachable and truly respectable characters in the country. On losing his Process, the Muse overheard him at his devotions as follows—

> "O thou that in the heavens does dwell!"

In Burns's autograph.

[Stanza iv., lines 4 and 6, read—

> "In burning lakes."
> "Chained to their stakes."]

XII.

Epigram—On Capt. F Grose—Antiquarian—see page 8ᵗʰ—

> "The devil got notice that Grose was a dying."

In Burns's autograph.

[The last line reads—

> "I'll want him ere take such a damnable load!"]

XIII.

Additional stanza to song, page 19th. [IX.]

"Awa', thou flaunting god o' day,"

In Burns's autograph.

XIV.

Copy of a letter from Mr. Burns to Doctor Moor.

An Amanuensis; corrected by Burns.

"Sir, - For some time past I have been rambling," etc.

[There are various alterations and additions in this long autobiographical letter, when compared with the version in Cunningham's edition. It is dated Mauchline, 2nd August, 1787.]

Note in Burns's autograph—

"Know all whom it may concern, that I, the Author, am not answerable for the false spelling and injudicious punctuation in the foregoing transcript of my letter to Dr. Moore. I have something generous in my temper that cannot bear to see or hear the Absent wronged, and I am very much hurt to observe that in several instances the transcriber has injured and mangled the proper name and principal title of a Personage of the very first distinction in all that is valuable among men, Antiquity, abilities, and power; (Virtue, everybody knows, is an obsolete business) I mean, the Devil. Considering that the Transcriber was one of the Clergy, an order that owe the very bread they eat to the said Personage's exertions, the affair was absolutely unpardonable.—Ro. B."

XV.

When Captain Grose was at Friar's Carse, in the summer of 1790, collecting materials for his Scottish Antiquities, he applied to Mr. Burns, then living in the neighbourhood, to write him an account of the Witches' meetings at Aloway Church, near Ayr, who complied with his request, and wrote for him the following poem :—

Tam o' Shanter.   A Tale.

"When chapmen billies leave the street."

An Amanuensis, corrected by Burns.

[The four lines (originally printed in Grose's *Antiquities of Scotland,* but afterwards omitted),

"Three Lawyers' tongues," etc.

appear in this copy.]

XVI.

On the death of Sir James Hunter Blair.

"The lamp of day with ill-presaging glare."

An Amanuensis.

Note in Burns's autograph—

"The Performance is but mediocre, but my grief was sincere. The last time I saw the worthy, public spirited man—A man he was ! How few of the two-legged breed that pass for such, deserve the designation !—he pressed my hand, and asked me with the most friendly warmth if it was in his power to serve me; and if so, that I would oblidge him by telling him how.   I had nothing to ask of him ; but if ever a child of his should be so unfortunate as to be under the necessity of asking anything of so poor a man as I am, it may not be in my power to grant it, but, by G——- I shall try ! ! ! "

XVII.

Written on the blank leaf of a Copy of the first Edition of my Poems, which I presented to an Old Sweetheart, then married.

"Once fondly loved, and still remembered dear."

An Amanuensis.

Note in Burns's autograph—

> " 'T was the girl I mentioned in my letter to Dr. Moore, where I speak of taking the sun's altitude. Poor Peggy! Her husband is my old acquaintance, and a most worthy fellow. When I was taking leave of my Carrick relations, intending to go to the West Indies, when I took farewell of her, neither she nor I could speak a syllable. Her husband escorted me three miles on my road, and we both parted with tears."

XVIII.

On reading in a newspaper the death of J. M'Leod Esquire, brother to Miss Isabella M'Leod, a particular friend of the author.

"Sad thy tale thou idle page."

An Amanuensis.

Note in Burns's autograph—

> "This poetic compliment, what few poetic compliments are, was from the heart."

XIX.

Epitaph on a Friend.

"An honest man here lies at rest."

An Amanuensis.

XX.

The humble petition of Bruar Water to the Noble Duke of Athole.

Bruar Falls are the finest in the country, but not a bush about them, which spoils much their beauty.

"My Lord, I know your noble ear."

An Amanuensis.

[Stanza vi., line 3, reads —

"The bairdie, Music's youngest child."]

Note in Burns's autograph—

"God, who knows all things, knows how my heart achs with the throes of gratitude, whenever I recollect my reception at the noble house of Athole."

XXI.

Extempore Epistle to Mr. M'Adam of Craigengillan (wrote in Nanse Tinnock's, Mauchline), in answer to an obliging letter he sent in the commencement of my poetic career.

"Sir, o'er a gill I gat your card."

An Amanuensis.

XXII.

On scaring some Waterfowl in Loch Turit, a wild scene among the wilds of Oughtertyre.

" Why, ye tenants of the lake."

An Amanuensis.

[Lines 13, 14, read—

" Conscious blushing for my kind,
Soon, too soon your fears I find."]

Note in Burns's autograph—

" This was the production of a solitary forenoon's walk from Oughtertyre House. I lived there, Sir William's guest, for two or three weeks, and was much flattered by my hospitable reception. What a pity that the mere emotions of gratitude are so impotent in this world ! 'Tis lucky that, as we are told,. they will be of some avail in the world to come."

XXIII.

Written in the Hermitage at Taymouth.

" Admiring nature in her wildest grace."

An Amanuensis.

Note in Burns's autograph—

" I wrote this with my pencil over the chimney-piece in the parlour of the Inn at Kenmore, at the outlet of Loch Tay."

XXIV.

Written at the Fall of Fyers.

"Among the heathy hills and ragged woods."

An Amanuensis.

Note in Burns's autograph—

"I composed these lines standing on the brink of the hideous caldron below the waterfall."

XXV.

Written by Somebody on the window of an inn at Stirling on seeing the royal palace in ruins.

"Here Stuarts once in triumph reigned."

An Amanuensis.

[Two unpublished lines (5 and 6) run—

"Fallen indeed, and to the earth,
Whence grovelling reptiles take their birth."]

Note in Burns's autograph—

"These imprudent lines were answered, very petulantly, by somebody, I believe a Rev. Mr. Hamilton! In a MSS., where I met with the answer, I wrote below:—

"With Esop's lion, Burns says, sore I feel
Each other blow, but d—mn that ass's heel!"

XXVI.

Epistle to Robt Graham, Esq., of Fintry, on the election -for the Dumfries string of boroughs, Anno 1790.

" Fintry, my stay in worldly strife."

In Burns's autograph.

[In the last stanza but one is this variation :

" For your poor friend, the Bard, afar
He hears and sees the distant war."]

XXVII.

A Poet's welcome to his love-begotten daughter, the first instance that entitled him to the venerable appellation of Father.

" Thou's welcome, Wean ! Mischanter fa' me."

In Burns's autograph.

[Some variations in stanza i. :

" Thou's welcome, Wean ! Mischanter fa' me,
If thoughts o' thee, or yet thy Mamie,
Shall ever daunton me or awe me,
    My bonie lady ;
Or if I blush when thou shalt ca' me
    Tyta or daddie."

Stanza ii.

" Tho' now they name me," etc.

Stanza iii. (unpublished).

> "Welcome! my bonie, sweet, wee Dochter!
> Tho' ye come here a wee unsought for,
> And tho' your comin I hae fought for,
>   Baith Kirk and Queir;
> Yet, by my faith, ye're no unwrought for,
>   That I shall swear!"

Stanza iv.

> "The image o' my bonie Betty,
>   As fatherly I kiss and daut thee," etc.

Stanza v.

> "Sweet fruit," etc.

Stanza vi. (unpublished).

> "Tho' I should be the waur bestead,
> Thou's be as braw and bienly clad,
> And thy young years as nicely bred
>   Wi' education,
> As ony brat o' Wedlock's bed,
>   In a' thy station.

Stanza vii. (much altered).

> "For if thou be, what I wad hae thee,
> And tak the counsel I shall gie thee,
> I'll never rue my trouble wi' thee,
>   The cost nor shame o't,
> But be a loving Father to thee,
>   And brag the name o't."

This ends the poem.]

XXVIII.

"The five Carlins—a Ballad."

" There was five Carlins in the South."

In Burns's autograph.

.   [There is a slight variation in the arrangement of one or two stanzas.]

XXIX.

Extempore, nearly.

On the birth of Mons[r] Henri, posthumous child to a Mons[r] Henri, a Gentleman of family and fortune from Switzerland; who died in three days illness, leaving his lady, a sister of Sir Thos. Wallace, in her sixth month of this her first child. The Lady and her Family were particular friends of the Author. The child was born in November —90.

"Sweet Floweret, pledge o' meikle love."

In Burns's autograph.

XXX.

Birthday Ode.—31st December, 1787.

"Afar th' illustrious Exile roams."

An Amanuensis.

[A portion of this Ode was given by Dr. Currie, who observes that in the first part of it there is some beautiful imagery, which the poet afterwards interwove in " The Chevalier's Lament."

It appears that the Jacobites in Edinburgh were in the habit of celebrating the anniversary of Charles Edward's birthday, on the 31st of each December.   Mr. Scott Douglas believes that Burns prepared this Ode for the anniversary held in 1787, though he was himself unable to be present, as he was then laid up, by an accident, at Mr. Cruikshank's house.

Here transcribed.]

XXXI.

Ode, sacred to the memory of Mrs. O., of A.   (Burns adds, " *Mrs. Oswald, of Auchencrue.*")

"Dweller in yon dungeon dark."

An Amanuensis.

XXXII.

Extempore—to Mr. Gavin Hamilton.

"To you, Sir, this summons I 've sent."

An Amanuensis.

[This poem is not included in the Kilmarnock edition, but it appears in that of Mr. Alexander Smith.]

XXXIII.

Lament of Mary Queen of Scots.

" Now Nature hangs her mantle green."

An Amanuensis.

XXXIV.

Epistle to Robt Graham, Esq., of Fintry, requesting a favor.

" When Nature her great Master-piece designed."

An Amanuensis.

[There are some slight variations.

Lines 4, 5 —

" She forms of various stuff the various Man.
The Useful Many first, she calls them forth."

Line 34—

" Admired and praised—and there the wages ends."

Lines 43–46—

" Viewing the propless Climber of Mankind,
She cast about a standard-tree to find ;
In pity for his helpless woodbine-state,
She clasped his tendrils round the truly Great."]

XXXV.

Jeremiah 15th ch., 10 v.

" Ah, woe is me, my Mother dear ! "

In Burns's autograph.

> [This poem was printed in Vol. II., p. 391, of the Kilmarnock
> edition ; but Mr. Scott Douglas, the editor, believed it to have been
> written by Hogg, in whose Memoir of Burns it first appeared. As
> this version varies somewhat from that already in print, I tran-
> scribe it.]

XXXVI. –VII.

From Clarinda, on Mr. B—'s saying that he had nothing else
to do.

" When first you saw Clarinda's charms."

Answer to the foregoing.   Extempore.

" When dear Clarinda, matchless fair."

Both in Burns's autograph.

> [Here transcribed as being unpublished.
>
> Is it possible that the former poem is also Burns's own compo-
> sition ?   The story of Burns's Platonic affection for Clarinda (Mrs.
> M'Lehose) is well known.]

XXXVIII.

On the death of the late Lord President Dundas.

" Lone on the bleaky hills, the straying flocks."

In Burns's autograph.

[Lines 33, 34, read—

" Ye dark, waste hills, ye brown, unsightly plains,
Congenial scenes ! ye soothe my mournful strains."]

XXXIX.

The Whistle—A Ballad.

" I sing of a whistle, a whistle of worth."

In Burns's autograph.

XL.

A new psalm for the Chapel of Kilmarnock.   On the thanks giving day for His Majesty's recovery.

" O sing a new song to the L——! "

In Burns's autograph.

[This appears in the Kilmarnock, but not in Alexander Smith's edition.]

XLI.

A ballad on the heresy of Dr. M'Gill, in Ayr.

"Orthodox ! orthodox ! wha believe in John Knox."

In Burns's autograph.

[There are several alterations (chiefly in arrangement of stanzas) from the current version.

    Stanza i.

           "Orthodox, orthodox."

    Stanza ii.

        (1) "Doctor Mac, Doctor Mac."

    Stanza iii.

        (2) "D'rymple mild, D'rymple mild."

    Stanza iv.

           "Calvin's sons, Calvin's sons."

    Stanza v.

        (3) "Rumble John, Rumble John."

    Stanza vi.

        (4) "Simper James, Simper James."

    Stanza vii.

        (5) "Andrew Gowk, Andrew Gowk."

    Stanza viii.

        (6) "Poet Willy, Poet Willy."

    Stanza ix.

        (7) "Barr Steenie, Barr Steenie."

    Stanza x.

        (8) "Jamie Goose, Jamie Goose."

Stanza xi. (unpublished); the stanza "David Bluster" appears to have been substituted for this.

> (9) " Davie Rant, Davie Rant, in a face like a saunt,
>   And a heart that wad poison a hog,
> Raise an impudent roar, like a breaker lee shore,
>   Or the Kirk will be tint in a bog."

Stanza xii.

> (10) " Daddy Auld, Daddy Auld."

Stanza xiii.

> (11) " Muirland Jock, Muirland Jock."

Stanza xiv.

> (12) " Cessnock side, Cessnock side."
> This stanza is the one usually printed, " Irvine-side, Irvine-side."

Stanza xv.

> " Poet Burns, Poet Burns."

Burns has added foot-notes.

1. Dr. M'gill, Ayr.   2. Dr. Dalrymple, Ayr.

3. John Russel, Kilmarnock.

4. James M'kindlay, Kilm^{ck}.

5. Dr. Andrew Mitchel, Monkton.

6. Will$^{m.}$ Peebles, in Newton-upon-Ayr, a poetaster, who, among many other things, published an ode on the Centenary of the Revolution, in which was the line,

> " And bound in Liberty's endearing chain."

7. Stephen Young, Barr.

8. Jas. Young, in New Cumnock, who had lately been foiled in an ecclesiastical prosecution against a Lieut. Mitchel.

9. David Grant, Ochiltree.

10. William Auld, Mauchlin ; for the Clerk, see "Holy Willie's Prayer."

11. John Shepherd, Muirkirk.   12. George Smith, Galston.]

XLII.

To Robert Graham, Esq., of Fintry, on receiving a favour.

"I call no goddess to inspire my strains."

In Burns's autograph.

XLIII.

Written in a wrapper enclosing a letter to Capt. Grose, to be left with Mr. Cardonnel, Antiquarian.—Tune, "Sir John Malcolm."

"Ken ye ought o' Captain Grose?"

In Burns's autograph.

[There is a slight variation in the arrangement of two stanzas.]

XLIV.

Fragment.

On Glenriddel's fox breaking his chain.

" Thou, Liberty, thou art my theme ! "

In Burns's autograph.

[Communicated by me to the *Athenæum* newspaper, April 25th, 1874, as previously unpublished.   Mr. E. C. Bigmore wrote in the following number of the *Athenæum*—

" In the spring of 1861, when in the employment of Messrs. Puttick and Simpson, I made a catalogue of a large collection of original MSS. of Burns's, among which was a copy of the poem, ' Thou, Liberty, thou art my theme.' . . . . The collection was subsequently sold by auction, and this particular poem was bought by Mr. Bell, of Manchester, for £3 5s."

Here transcribed.]

XLV.-

Lament for James, Earl of Glencairn.

" The wind blew hollow frae the hills."

In Burns's autograph.

[The last lines show some variation—

" The mother may forget the bairn,
    That smiles sae sweetly on her knee ;
But I'll remember good Glencairn,
    That a' that he has done for me."]

XLVI.

Epistle to Roland Graham, Esq., of Fintry.—5th Oct., 1791

"Late crippled of an arm, and now a leg."

In Burns's autograph.

XLVII.

Lines to Sir John Whitefoord, of Whitefoord, with a poem to the memory of Lord Glencairn.

"Thou, who thy honor as thy God rever'st."

In Burns's autograph.

XLVIII.

A Grace before dinner.   Extempore.

"O Thou, who kindly dost provide."

In Burns's autograph.

XLIX.

Epigram.

On being asked why God had made Miss Davies so little and Mrs. —— so big.

"Ask why God made the gem so small."

In Burns's autograph.

L.

On hearing it said that there was falsehood in Dr. B—b—ngt—n's very looks.

"That there is falsehood in his looks."

In Burns's autograph.

LI.

On Capt. W. R—dd—ck, of C—-rb—t—n.

"Light lay the earth on Billy's heart."

In Burns's autograph.

LII.

On W. Gr—h—m, Esq., of M—sskn—w.

"'Stop thief!' dame Nature called to Death."

In Burns's autograph.

[It has hitherto been generally supposed that these two savage epigrams were addressed to the same person, but to whom was never known. I cannot at all fill up the name of Mr. Graham's place, and it is doubtful whether the last letter is an "a," or a "w."]

LIII.

On Capt. L—sc—lls.

"When L—sc—lls thought fit from this world to depart."

In Burns's autograph.

[Unpublished and transcribed.]

LIV.

Pinned to Mrs. W—lt—r R—dd—ll's carriage.

"If you rattle along like your Mistress s tongue."

In Burns's autograph.

LV.

Epitaph on J—hn B—shby.

"Here lies John B—shby, *honest man.*"

In Burns's autograph.

LVI.

On J—hn M—r—ne, laird of L—gg—n.

"When M—r—ne, deceased, to the devil went down."

In Burns's autograph.

[The name here has hitherto been left an entire blank.]

LVII.

On the laird of C—rd—nn—ss.

"Bless J—s—s Chr—st, O C—rd—nn—ss."

In Burns's autograph.

POEMS.

POEMS.

I.

Epistle to John Goldie in Kilmarnock, author of " The Gospel Recovered."—August, 1785.

O Gowdie, terror o' the whigs,
  Dread o' blackcoats and reverend wigs ! .
Sour Bigotry on his last legs
        Girns and looks back,
Wishing the ten Egyptian plagues
        May seize you quick.

Poor gapin, glowrin Superstition !
  Waes me, she 's in a sad condition :
Fye ! bring Black Jock,* her state-physician,
        To see her water :
Alas there 's ground for great suspicion
        She 'll ne'er get better.

Enthusiasm 's past redemption,
  Gane in a gallopin consumption :
Not a' her quacks wi' a' their gumption
        Can ever mend her ;
Her feeble pulse gies strong presumption
        She 'll soon surrender.

* The Rev. J. R—ss—l, Kilm^{ck}.

Auld Orthodoxy lang did grapple
For every hole to get a stapple ;
But now, she fetches at the thrapple
And fights for breath ;
Haste, gie her name up in the chapel, *
Near unto death.

It 's you and Taylor † are the chief
To blame for a' this black mischief ;
But could the L—d's ain folk get leave,
A toom tar barrel
And twa red peats wad bring relief
And end the quarrel.

[Unpublished stanza.]

For me, my skill 's but very sma',
And skill in Prose I 've nane ava ;
But quietlenswise, between us twa,
Weel may ye speed ;
And tho' they sud you sair misca',
Ne'er fash your head.

[Unpublished stanza.]

E'en swinge the dogs ; and thresh them sicker !
The mair they squeel ay chap the thicker ;
And still 'mang hands a hearty bicker
O' something stout ;
It gars an Owther's pulse beat quicker,
And helps his wit.

---

* Chapel—Mr. Russel's kirk.   † Taylor—Dr. Taylor, of Norwich.

[Stanzas published as separate Poem.]

There 's naething like the honest nappy ;
　　Whare 'll ye e'er see men sae happy,
　　Or women sonsie, saft and sappy,
　　　　'Tween morn and morn,
　　As them wha like to taste the drappie
　　　　In glass or horn.

I 've seen me daez't upon a time,
　　I scarce could wink or see a styme ;
　　Just ae hauf mutchkin does me prime,
　　　　(Ought less, is little)
　　Then back I rattle on the rhyme,
　　　　As gleg 's a whittle.

I am, etc.

II.

Ode to the departed Regency Bill.—1789.

Daughter of Chaos' doting years,
Nurse of ten thousand hopes and fears ;
Whether thy airy, unsubstantial Shade
(The rights of sepulture now duly paid)
Spread abroad its hideous form
On the roaring Civil Storm,
Deafening din and warring rage
Factions wild with factions wage ;
Or under-ground, deep-sunk, profound,
Among the demons of the earth,
With groans that make the mountains shake,
Thou mourn thy ill-starred, blighted birth ;
Or in the uncreated Void,
Where seeds of future-being fight,
With lightened step thou wander wide,
To greet thy Mother—Ancient Night,
And as each jarring, monster mass is past,
Fond recollect what once thou wast :
In manner due, beneath this sacred oak,
Hear, Spirit, hear ! thy presence I invoke !
By a Monarch's heaven-struck fate !
By a disunited State !
By a generous Prince's wrongs !
By a Senate's strife of tongues !
By a Premier's sullen pride,
Louring on the changing tide !

By dread Thurlow's powers to awe,
Rhetoric, blasphemy and law !
By the turbulent ocean,
A Nation's commotion !
By the harlot-caresses
Of borough addresses ! .
By days, few and evil !
Thy portion, poor devil !
By Power, Wealth, Show ! the gods by men adored !
By nameless Poverty ! their hell abhorred !
By all they hope ! By all they fear !
Hear ! ! ! And Appear ! ! !

Stare not on me, thou ghastly Power ;
Nor grim with chained defiance lour :
No Babel-structure would *I* build
Where, Order exiled from his native sway,
Confusion may the REGENT-sceptre wield,
While all would rule and none obey :
Go, to the world of Man relate
The story of thy sad, eventful fate ;
And call Presumptuous Hope to hear,
And bid him check his blind career ;
And tell the sore-prest sons of Care,
Never, never to despair !

Paint CHARLES's speed on wings of fire,
The object of his fond desire,
Beyond his boldest hopes, at hand :
Paint all the triumph of the Portland Band :
Mark how they lift the joy-exulting voice ;
And how their numerous Creditors rejoice :
But just as hopes to warm enjoyment rise,
Cry, CONVALESCENCE ! and the vision flies.

Then next pourtray a darkening twilight gloom,
   Eclipsing, sad, a gay, rejoicing morn,
While proud Ambition to th' untimely tomb
   By gnashing, grim, despairing fiends is borne :
Paint ruin, in the shape of high D——— *
   Gaping with giddy terror o'er the brow ;
In vain he struggles, the fates behind him press,
   And clamorous hell yawns for her prey below :
How fallen That, whose pride late scaled the skies !
And This, like Lucifer, no more to rise !
   Again pronounce the powerful word;
See Day, triumphant from the night, restored.

Then know this truth, ye Sons of Men !
   (Thus end thy moral tale)
Your darkest terrors may be vain,
   Your brightest hopes may fail.

[* Dundas ?]

III.

*Birthday Ode.—*31*st December,* 1787.

(The portion previously published is printed in Italics.)

Afar the illustrious Exile roams
   Whom kingdoms on this day should hail :
   An inmate in the casual shed,
   On transient pity's bounty fed,
Haunted by busy memory's bitter tale !
   Beasts of the forest have their savage homes,
   But He who should imperial purple wear,
Owns not the lap of earth where rests his royal head !
   His wretched refuge, dark despair,
   While ravening wrongs and woes pursue ;
   And distant far the faithful few
   Who would his sorrows share.
   False flatterer, hope, away !
Nor think to lure us as in days of yore :
   We solemnize this sorrowing natal day,
   To prove our loyal truth—we can no more;
   And owning Heaven's mysterious sway,
   Submissive, low, adore.
   Ye honored, mighty Dead !
Who nobly perished in the glorious cause,
   Your KING, your Country, and her laws !
   From great DUNDEE, who smiling Victory led,
   And fell a Martyr in her arms,
   (What breast of northern ice but warms !)
   To bold BALMERINO'S undying name,
   Whose soul of fire, lighted at Heaven's high flame,
Deserves the proudest wreath departed heroes claim :

r

Not unrevenged your fate shall lie,
It only lags, the fatal hour;
Your blood shall with incessant cry,
Awake at last th' unsparing Power.
As from the cliff, with thundering course,
The snowy ruin smokes along,
With doubling speed, and gathering force,
Till deep it, crushing, whelms the cottage in the vale;
So VENGEANCE' arm, ensanguined, strong,
Shall with resistless might assail :
Usurping B———ck's pride shall lowly lay,
And STEWART'S wrongs and yours, with tenfold weight, repay.
PERDITION, baleful child of night !
Rise and revenge the injured right
    Of ST— ·W—RT'S royal race :
Lead on the unmuzzled hounds of hell,
Till all the frighted echoes tell
The blood-notes of the chase !
Full on the quarry point their view ;
Full on the base usurping crew,
The tools of faction, and the nation's curse !
Hark, how the cry grows on the wind ;
They leave the lagging gale behind ;
Their savage fury, pitiless, they pour ;
With murdering eyes already they devour :
See B———ck spent, a wretched prey ;
His life one poor despairing day,
Where each avenging hour still ushers in a worse !
Such havock, howling all abroad,
    Their utter ruin bring ;
The base apostates to their GOD,
    Or rebels to their KING.

IV.

Jeremiah, 15th Chapter, 10 V.

Ah, woe is me, my Mother dear !
  A man of strife ye've born me :
For sair contention I maun bear,
  They hate, revile, and scorn me.

I ne'er could lend on bill or band,
  That five per cent might blest me ;
And borrowing, on the tither hand,
  The de'il a ane wad trust me.

Yet I, a coin-denièd wight,
  By Fortune quite discarded,
Ye see how I am, day and night,
  By lad and lass blackguarded !

V.

From Clarinda,* on Mr. B———'s saying that he had "nothing else to do."

When first you saw Clarinda's charms,
    What raptures in your bosom grew !
Her heart was shut to love's alarms,
    But then—you 'd nothing else to do.

Apollo oft had lent his harp,
    But now 'twas strung from Cupid's bow ;
You sung, it reached Clarinda's heart,
    She wish'd—you 'd nothing else to do.

Fair Venus smil'd, Minerva frown'd,
    Cupid observ'd, the arrow flew :
Indifference (ere a week went round)
    Shew'd—you 'd had nothing else to do.

Christmas Eve.   CLARINDA.

Note by Burns.

* This lady was the authoress of two songs, Nos. 186 and 190, in the 2nd vol. of Johnson's *Scots Musical Museum.*

VI.

Answer to the foregoing.   Extempore.

When dear Clarinda, matchless fair,
  First struck Sylvander's raptured view,
He gaz'd, he listen'd to despair,
  Alas ! 't was all he dar'd to do.

Love, from Clarinda's heavenly eyes
  Transfixed his bosom thro' and thro' ;
But still in Friendship's guarded guise,
  For more the demon fear'd to do.

That heart, already more than lost,
  The imp beleaguer'd all perdue ;
For frowning Honor kept his post,
  To meet that frown he shrunk to do.

His pangs the Bard refused to own,
  Tho' half he wish'd Clarinda knew :
But Anguish wrung th' unweeting groan—
  Who blames what frantic Pain must do ?

That heart, where motely follies blend,
  Was sternly still to Honor true :
To prove Clarinda's fondest friend,
  Was what a Lover sure might do.

The Muse his ready quill employ'd,
  No dearer bliss he could pursue ;
That bliss Clarinda cold deny'd,—
  " Send word by Charles how you do ! "

The chill behest disarm'd his muse
  Till Passion all impatient grew :
He wrote, and hinted for excuse,
  " 'T was 'cause he 'd nothing else to do."

But by those hopes I have above !
  And by those faults I dearly rue !
The deed, the boldest mark of love,
  For thee that deed I dare to do !

O, could the Fates but name the price,
  Would bless me with your charms and you !
With frantic joy I 'd pay it thrice,
  If human art and power could do !

Then take, Clarinda, friendship's hand,
  (Friendship, at least, I may avow ;)
And lay no more your chill command,
  I 'll write, whatever I 've to do.

                    SYLVANDER.

VII.

A Fragment.—On Glenriddel's Fox breaking his Chain.

Thou, Liberty, thou art my theme ;
Not such as idle Poets dream,
Who trick thee up a Heathen goddess
That a fantastic cap and rod has ;
Such stale conceits are poor and silly ;
I paint thee out, a Highland filly,
A sturdy, stubborn, handsome dapple,
As sleek 's a mouse, as round 's an apple,
That when thou pleasest can do wonders ;
But when thy luckless rider blunders,
Or if thy fancy should demur there,
Wilt break thy neck ere thou go further.

These things premis'd, I sing a fox,
Was caught among his native rocks,
And to a dirty kennel chained,
How he his liberty regained.

Glenriddel, a Whig without a stain,
A Whig in principle and grain,
Couldst thou enslave a free-born creature,
A native denizen of nature ?
How couldst thou, with a heart so good,
(A better ne'er was sluiced with blood)
Nail a poor devil to a tree,
That ne'er did harm to thine or thee ?

The staunchest Whig Glenriddel was,
Quite frantic in his Country's cause ;
And oft was Reynard's prison passing,
And with his brother Whigs canvassing
The Rights of Men, the Powers of Women,
With all the dignity of Freemen.

Sir Reynard daily heard debates
Of Princes', kings', and Nations' fates ;
With many rueful, bloody stories
Of tyrants, Jacobites, and tories :
From liberty how angels fell,
That now are galley-slaves in hell ;
How Nimrod first the trade began
Of binding Slavery's chains on man ;
How fell Semiramis, G—d d—mn her!
Did first with sacrilegious hammer,
(All ills till then were trivial matters)
For Man dethroned forge hen-peck fetters ;
How Xerxes, that abandoned tory,
Thought cutting throats was reaping glory,
Until the stubborn Whigs of Sparta
Taught him great Nature's Magna Charta ;
How mighty Rome her fiat hurl'd,
Resistless o'er a bowing world,
And kinder than they did desire,
Polished mankind with sword and fire :
With much too tedious to relate
Of Ancient and of Modern date,
But ending, still, how Billy Pit,
(Unlucky boy!) with wicked wit,
Has gagg'd old Britain, drained her coffer,
As butchers bind and bleed a heifer.—

Thus wily Reynard, by degrees,
In kennel listening at his ease,
Suck'd in a mighty stock of knowledge,
As much as some folks at a college.—
Knew Britain's rights and constitution,
Her aggrandisement, diminution,
How fortune wrought us good from evil ;
Let no man, then, despise the devil,
As who should say, I ne'er can need him ;
Since we to scoundrels owe our freedom.—

VIII.

On Capt^u. L—sc—lls.

When L—sc—lls thought fit from this world to depart,
Some friends warmly spoke of embalming his heart:
A bystander whispers, pray do'nt make so much on't,
The subject is poison—no reptile will touch it.

MEMORANDA

CAPT. ROBERT RIDDELL of GLENRIDDELL,

(COMMUNICATED BY W. SCOTT DOUGLAS.)

WHEN Burns took up his abode at Ellisland (in the summer of 1788), his nearest neighbour to the west was Capt. Riddell, Friars' Carse; the residence of this gentleman was about a mile from Burns' farm house, both being pleasantly situated on the banks of the Nith. Riddell was an Antiquary of some note, and an agreeable friend, and Burns no sooner came to settle at Ellisland than he was welcomed to Friars' Carse. So early as the 16th Sept. of that year, the Poet, in writing to a friend, inclosed a lyric commencing —

"The day returns, my bosom burns,"

which (he says) "I made to an air that a musical gentleman of my acquaintance — Capt. Riddell of Glenriddell — composed for the anniversary of his wedding day." In a head-note to a printed copy of that production, the Poet remarks — "This song I composed in compliment to one of the happiest and worthiest married couples in the world, Robt. Riddell Esq. of Glenriddell, and his lady. At their fireside I have enjoyed more pleasant evenings than at all the houses of fashionable people in this country put together; and to their kindness and hospitality I am indebted for many of the happiest hours of my life."

The worthy proprietor of Friars' Carse had given Burns a key admitting him to the grounds, and it seems to have been one of the chief delights of the Poet's life, at this period, to wander there, and muse in a decorated cot or hermitage, which the owner had erected. Here, on 28th June, 1788, he composed, under the character of a religious recluse, his *Verses on Friars' Carse Hermitage*, beginning —

> "Thou whom chance may hither lead."

In the Mansion, on 16th October, 1789, took place a Bacchanalian contest, which makes a conspicuous figure in the Poems of Burns, the object being the possession of a certain ebony Whistle which had been won by an ancestor of Sir Robt. Lawrie, of Maxwellton, from a Danish champion of Bacchus, who came to Scotland in the train of Queen Anne, of Denmark, consort of King James VI. The three claret-champions on the present occasion were Capt. Riddell (the host); Mr. Ferguson, of Craigdarroch; and Sir Robert Lawrie, of Maxwellton. Mr. Ferguson was the victor, and the Whistle is still in the possession of his family. Burns, by pre-arrangement, celebrated the contest very promptly, and in a very felicitous manner; but although he adopts the poetic license to sing —

> "A bard was selected to witness the fray,
> And tell future ages the feats of the day,"

no fact can be more certain than that he was not present at the claret-encounter.

Besides the two volumes (one of Letters and the other of Poems) which Burns transcribed for preservation in Capt. Riddell's library, and which are now happily preserved in the Athenæum Library of Liverpool, he enriched with manuscript notes an interleaved copy of the first four parts of *Johnson Scot's Musical Museum*. These Notes were carefully published by Cromek, in 1810. It also appears, from the Poet's correspondence, that shortly after Mr. Riddell's death, in April, 1794, the Poet applied to that gentleman's relatives, begging that the volume of Manuscript Poetry above referred to might be returned to him or destroyed. The following passage in his letter is interesting as bearing on the contents of the volume now presented to the public :—

"You know that at the wish of my late friend, I made a collection of all my trifles in verse which I had ever written. They are many of them local, some of them puerile and silly, and all of them unfit for the public eye. As I have some little fame at stake — a fame that I trust may live when the hate of those who 'watch for my halting' and the contumelious sneer of those whom accident has made my superiors, will, with themselves, be gone to the region of oblivion. I am uneasy now for the fate of those manuscripts. Will Mrs. Riddel have the goodness to destroy them, or return them to me ? As a pledge of friendship they were bestowed ; and that circumstance, indeed, was all their merit."

The only other reference to this MS. volume in the Bard's printed correspondence is in a note addressed to Captain Riddell, dating from Ellisland in 1789. He there says —

"If my poems which I have transcribed, and mean still to transcribe, into your book, were equal to the grateful respect and high esteem I bear for the gentleman to whom I present them, they would be the finest poems in any language. As they are, they will at least be a testimony with what sincerity I have the honour to be Sir, your devoted, humble servant,

                                                          R. B."

Burns had few opportunities of meeting Captain Riddell, after giving up his farm at Ellisland and removing with his family to Dumfries, in December, 1791 ; but in that town he soon contracted a lively intimacy with a younger brother of the Laird of Glenriddell, Mr. Walter Riddell of Woodley Park, near Dumfries. That gentleman had been long resident in the West Indies, where he possessed an estate, and had just then returned to his native country with a young, handsome, and very accomplished wife, a daughter of the Governor of Berbice. This lady having a taste for literature and science, delighted in the society of men of talent, and the vivid genius of Burns having attracted her, the Poet became a frequent visitor at Woodley Park. An unfortunate quarrel having occurred between the Poet and Mr. Walter Riddell, about Christmas time of 1793, which is glanced at in the letter first above quoted, the worthy Laird of Glenriddell espoused the cause of his brother, and thereby those fast friends were disunited when Captain Riddell's death occurred within a few months thereafter. When that event happened, the Poet, remembering only his friend's worth and kindness, immediately penned and published an elegiac Sonnet on the occasion :—

SONNET

On the Death of Robert Riddell Esq. of Friars' Carse.

"No more, ye warblers of the wood! no more;
   Nor pour your descant grating on my soul:
   Thou, young-eyed Spring! gay in thy verdant stole,
More welcome were to me grim Winter's wildest roar.
How can ye charm, ye flowers! with all your dyes?
   Ye blow upon the sod that wraps my friend!
   How can I to the tuneful strain attend?
That strain flows round th' untimely tomb where Riddell lies.

Yes, pour, ye warblers! pour the notes of woe,
   And soothe the Virtues weeping on this bier:
   The Man of Worth—and hath not left his peer—
Is in his 'narrow house' for ever darkly low.
   Thee, Spring! again with joy shall others greet;
   Me memory of my loss will only meet."

Mr. Walter Riddell seems to have been a fast-living squire. Woodley Park was advertised for sale on 1st April, 1794, and he having inherited Friars' Carse from his brother, that estate was in like manner advertised in June of same year.

Mrs. Walter Riddell did for Burns, immedaitely after his decease, what the Poet had done for her relative, the Laird of Carse. She composed and published one of the finest panegyrics on the genius and character of the departed Bard that has ever been penned. On becoming a widow, about the close of last century, she removed to London, and married an Irish gentleman about Court, named Fletcher, and died in State apartments at Hampton Palace in 1820.

Friars' Carse was purchased by a Captain Smith, who suffered the "Hermitage" to fall into decay. Burns had paid it a visit after Glenriddell's death, and inscribed on one of its panes these lines —

> " To Riddell, much lamented man,
>   This ivied cot was dear;
> Wanderer, dost value matchless worth?
>   This ivied cot revere."

Friars' Carse subsequently became the property of Mrs. Crichton, widow of him who founded the "Crichton Institution," Dumfries.

LIVERPOOL :

GILBERT G. WALMSLEY, PRINTER,

LORD STREET.

www.ingramcontent.com/pod-product-compliance
Lightning Source LLC
Chambersburg PA
CBHW030859260626
47169CB00008B/2598